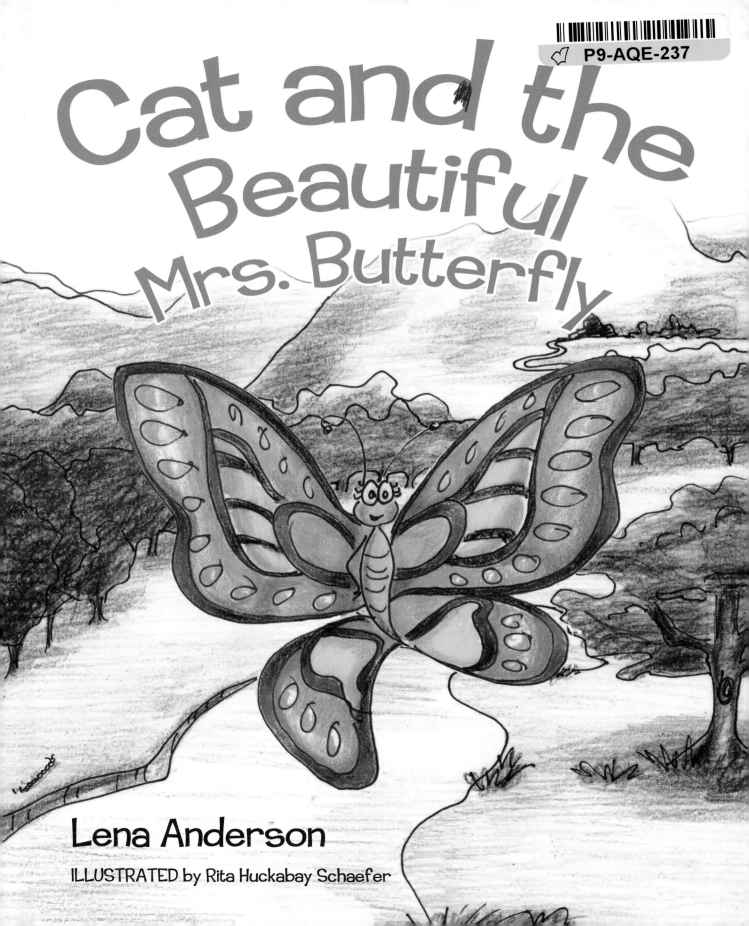

Cat and the Beautiful Mrs. Butterfly

Lena Anderson

ILLUSTRATED by Rita Huckabay Schaefer

Valerie is eight years old. Today, she rode the train by herself to visit her grandparents. Her grandparents live in Pinehurst, a little town a few miles from the city of Tomball where Valerie and her parents live.

Her trip was not long, but for Valerie, this trip was *different*.

You see, there is something special about the forest that grows behind Grandpa's property. Valerie has heard many wonderful stories from her dad about the forest and its creatures. She believes they are true, and Grandpa says they are.

It's not long before Valerie is in her room and looking out the window. She looks toward *Elf King Forest*.

She jumps when Pippen, Grandpa's dog, comes barking and running into her room.

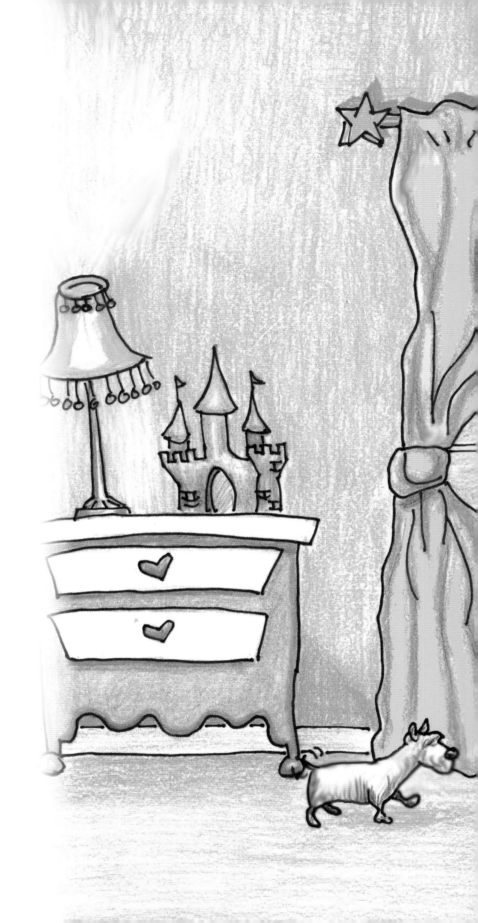

"Pippen! Pippen! I've missed you so much," she says to this dog who won't stop wagging his tail and licking her face.

She and Pippen have been friends since she was six years old. They are very glad to see each other again.

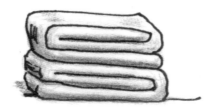

"Perhaps you can help him stay out of trouble," says Grandma as she enters the room with fresh sheets and blankets.

"That dog never stops chasing some critter or another into the forest," she says. "Why, yesterday morning, he chased a squirrel into the forest and didn't come home 'til almost suppertime!"

"That you can depend on," says Grandpa. "He will always come home for supper."

Everyone laughs, but Valerie begins to wonder, *What happens in the forest to keep him there for so long?*

That afternoon, as Valerie and Pippen play in the backyard, they spot a butterfly. The butterfly flies around them as though she wants attention.

She is so pretty, thinks Valerie as she marvels at the butterfly's many colors. *No wonder she's showing off.*

The butterfly begins to tease Pippen. First, she tickles him by landing on his ear, and then she brushes his nose with her wing. This makes Pippen sneeze! He is not a happy puppy.

When the butterfly flies off, Pippen chases after it. Valerie, not wanting to lose sight of Pippen or the beautiful butterfly, follows closely behind. Soon, they are at the edge of the forest.

"Stop, Pippen!" cries Valerie.

"This is as far as we are allowed to go, Pippen," she says.

Valerie and Pippen watch the butterfly fly in circles before entering the forest. Valerie knows they're not allowed in the forest alone, but Pippen doesn't. After all he is just a dog.

With a burst of speed, Pippen springs for an opening into *Elf King Forest.* Valerie stays close behind.

It's not long before Valerie knows she and Pippen are lost and in big trouble! She will worry about that later. Right now, she has to find their way back home.

"Pippen!" she cries. "See what you've done?" Her lips quiver as she speaks. "You just had to go after that butterfly!" she says. "I told you to stop, but no!" Then she adds, almost in a whisper, "And you got *us* lost."

In her heart, Valerie knows it's not Pippen's fault,
but Pippen doesn't. He hangs his head and lowers his
tail. Looking pitiful, Pippen follows behind Valerie not
wanting to lead anymore.

"We should have stayed on our side of the forest, Pippen," says Valerie. "The safe side." She looks around at the big trees and thick shrubs.

"And," she adds, "this is the weirdest forest I have ever seen. It's too quiet, and it somehow seems so sad."

Valerie looks at brown flowers and black trees with tan leaves. The rocks are mossy green and the creek has pale raspberry waters with white fish swimming in it. "Yuk!" she cries. "Pale orange frogs?"

Grandpa has told Valerie many stories about this forest. She knows things can be different here. They certainly are today.

Before Valerie has time to think about what is going on, Pippen begins to whine. Valerie turns to see why.

Out of a pale green bush walks a two-foot, light pink caterpillar with bright violet eyes. He has many hips, hands, and legs, and has two antennae that sit on the top of his shiny round head.

He walks boldly up to Valerie, and in his excitement, turns a little purple.

"Where did you find those colors?" he asks. "Where did you find that red and white on your shirt, the blue on your jeans, and the brown on your boots?"

Valerie just stares at him, unable to say a word. She has never seen or heard of a big, talking, pinkish-purple worm before. It takes her a moment to gather her thoughts.

"I'm so sorry," says the overgrown caterpillar. "I have no manners! No manners at all!" He wipes his many hands on his many hips. "My name is Cat," he says. "Cat the caterpillar. Get it?" he asks, as he offers several hands for Valerie to shake.

Valerie, who picks a hand to shake, thinks, *He has the biggest, prettiest eyes I have ever seen.*

Cat, feeling a little self-conscious, reminds Valerie, "My question, please. It's important, you understand."

"Why, the colors on my clothes have always been there," answers Valerie. "But what happened to this forest? Where are the colors?" she asks.

"They were here," she continues, "before we entered the forest, behind that beautiful butterfly."

"Mrs. Butterfly!" exclaims Cat. "Of course!" His arms fly up then down, landing on his many hips.

Slowly he says, "Mrs. Butterfly has taken our colors, again. She is such a selfish cocoon!" he shouts. "She is all wrapped up in herself."

He rubs his chin with one hand and is deep in thought, like a detective. Then, he turns his attention back to Valerie.

"Oh, please excuse my language," he says. "I would tell her myself, if she were here."

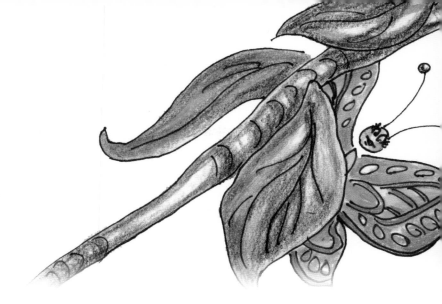

"That Mrs. Butterfly has become such a pest," says Cat. "She keeps taking our colors and then brags about how beautiful she looks.

"She's so full of it," says Cat as he begins to get all worked up. "Full of pride, that is," he explains. "Full of *pride*."

"How rude of her!" says Valerie.

"Ugly," says Cat. "I don't mind saying it. She's just plain ugly!"

Cat continues to rub his very round chin. He knows he is on his way to solving this mystery.

Pausing for a moment he explains, "The last time, Mrs. Butterfly hid our colors in a cave near the top of Hill Top Mountain where the creek begins."

"On the way up there, I was almost eaten by a gray raven that didn't seem to mind if he ever got his color back. I had to do a lot of talking.

"Nevertheless," he continues, "if it had not been for his wonderful wife, who likes to color coordinate everything, I don't know what would have happened to me."

"And, the time before," says Cat, "Mrs. Butterfly hid them in a beehive. Thanks to Bobo Bear, we got them back from the furious bees who thought we wanted their honey."

"Well, Bobo Bear did eat some of the honey. Now his nose is a bit tender."

"I'm afraid he won't help me again," says Cat. "Even though he says mauve is not his color."

"Oh, my," says Valerie, as she continues to listen to Cat.

Cat explains, because he is again willing to look for the colors, a fairy princess temporarily allows him to grow taller. In this way, he can get around faster and not be an easy target for hungry, unconcerned birds.

For a moment, Valerie wonders, *Who is this fairy princess?*

She then shifts her thoughts back to Cat and says, "You are a brave and selfless caterpillar. You have so much responsibility resting on your many little shoulders."

Cat blushes. He never thought twice about helping to find the colors. But now, he feels pretty proud of himself.

Finally, Valerie gives Cat the answer he is hoping for.

"I'll help you look for your colors," she says. "Perhaps then, you can help us find our way back home."

"I will, I will," answers Cat, glad to have help.

"We can start by climbing the tallest tree," says Valerie. "To see what we can see. There's a tall tree over there!"

"*Dullsville!*" says Cat. "That's all you'll see. *Dullsville!*"

As Valerie starts to climb the tree, Cat follows. Up they climb, while Pippen is content to watch from below.

Through the branches, at the top of the tree, Valerie sees a beautiful rainbow.

"That has to be the prettiest rainbow in the entire world," she tells Cat.

"Rainbow? What rainbow?" asks Cat. He looks toward the sky. His eyes follow the rainbow. Then suddenly he shouts, "Why, it's coming from Farmer Brown's barn!"

"Valerie, I think we found our colors," he says proudly.

Inside the barn, they find many cans of paint, but paint of a different sort. Valerie has never seen this type of paint before, but she knows it belongs to the forest.

"*Wow!* What shall we do now?" asks Valerie. "How do we get these colors back, and how do we get Mrs. Butterfly to behave herself?"

While they are talking, in flies Mrs. Butterfly through the open doors. Her colors are so bright that, for a moment, Cat, Pippen, and Valerie have to squint their eyes to see.

"If you have come to take the colors back," says the very annoyed Mrs. Butterfly, "I'll only hide them again."

Cat tries to make himself small to hide from Mrs. Butterfly's anger and steps behind Valerie. But Valerie stands her ground.

"Excuse me," says Valerie. "Why are you being a pest and taking what does not belong to you?"

"A *pest*?" asks Mrs. Butterfly, a little confused. "A pest is not what a beautiful butterfly wants to be."

"These colors do not belong to you!" says Valerie, with much authority in her voice.

Mrs. Butterfly argues, "But this way, everyone can see how beautiful I am without any doubt."

"Oh, *please*," answers Valerie in a smug voice. "All the creatures I have spoken to say you are a cocoon. They say you are all wrapped up in yourself."

Valerie looks at her fingernails on her left hand, and adds, "They say you act ugly, and ugly is all they see."

Cat, fearing Mrs. Butterfly will surely know it is he who has said these things, is now so embarrassed that he has turned another shade of pinkish-purple.

"Ugly is as ugly does," continues Valerie as she turns toward Cat, looking for his approval.

Instead, she finds him trembling and mumbling to himself.

"It wasn't me. It wasn't me. I didn't say that."

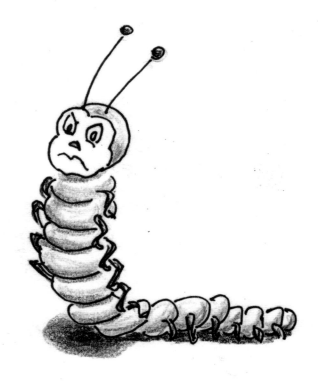

When Cat sees that Mrs. Butterfly has a tear in her eye, he again stands tall. He places his many hands on his many hips and puts on an unbelievable frown.

"Oh, dear. Is that really what they say?" Mrs. Butterfly asks. Then trying to compose herself, she adds, "Maybe I was being a cocoon and thought only of myself."

"I had no right to take those colors. And I do miss all of my friends.

"I'll put them back myself and I won't act ugly ever again," promises Mrs. Butterfly, and off she goes.